Carlo Likes Reading

Jessica Spanyol

WALKER BOOKS

AND SUBSIDIARIES

LONDON · BOSTON · SYDNEY

book

Carlo reads his bedroom.

Carlo reads his breakfast.

Carlo reads
the bathroom.

Carlo reads
Dad.

Carlo's mum reads to Carlo.

puppet

spider

Carlo's painting

rabbit

doll's-house

straw

stegosaurus

Crackers

drum

hen

robot

pig

cake

Carlo reads to Crackers the cat.

cloud

Carlo reads with
his friend Nevil.

wall

butterfly

puddle

flowerpot

watering-
can

ladybird

digger

bucket

worm

snail

baby's mum

balloon

Oper

Carlo reads
to a baby.

door

baby

pram

dummy

wheel

bakery

Price-list

pie   85P
tarts   23P
bread   47P

wedding cake

birthday cake

chocolate cake

bread

cherry pie

tarts

doughnuts

handle

Pigeon

sausage dogs

Carlo reads to some ducks.

Carlo reads at the market.

raindrop

bee

rose

sunflower

tulip

daisy

petal

Pete's dog

apples

Carlo's bag

Carlo likes
reading
very much.

And he loves
galloping.